Wind Says Good Night

Katy Rydell   *Illustrated by* David Jorgensen

Houghton Mifflin Company

Boston

www.hmco.com/trade

Library of Congress Cataloging-in-Publication Data
Rydell, Katy.
Wind says good night / Katy Rydell; illustrated by David Jorgensen.
p.   cm.
Summary: A child can't go to sleep until night wind sets events in motion affecting cloud,
earth, moon, moth, frog, cricket, and mockingbird; and quiet comes to the night.
RNF ISBN 0-395-60474-5   PAP ISBN 0-618-08585-8
[1. Bedtime — Fiction. 2. Night — Fiction.] I. Jorgensen, David, ill. II. Title.
PZ7.R9589Wi   1994
[E] — dc20   91-31675   CIP   AC

Printed in the United States of America
WOZ 10 9 8 7 6

For Katie and Lynsey —K. R.

For Joanne Mitchell and Elizabeth Beane —D. J.

It was late at night. All little children were in their beds, fast asleep. All except one.

The night wind brushed against a window. *"Shh-h-h,"* whispered the wind. "Go to sleep."

But the child could not fall asleep. Outside, on the branch of a tree, Mockingbird was singing.

"Mockingbird," said the night wind, "will you stop singing
   so the child can go to sleep?"

But Mockingbird loved to sing. Music spilled from deep in
his throat, as he sang of green woods, bright flowers, and
warm summer nights.
   "No," said Mockingbird, "I can't stop singing until
Cricket stops playing."

From the tall grass by the back steps came the cheerful ring
of Cricket's tune.

"Cricket," said the night wind, "will you stop playing
    so Mockingbird will stop singing
        so the child can go to sleep?"

But Cricket didn't want to stop playing. His toes were tapping,
his coattails flapping, as the melody flowed from his fiddle
strings.
    "No," said Cricket, "I can't stop playing until Frog stops
strumming."

"Frog," said the night wind, "will you stop strumming
so Cricket will stop playing
so Mockingbird will stop singing
so the child can go to sleep?"

But Frog was deep in the swing, lost in the beat, with a
night full of rhythm in his hands and feet.
    "No," said Frog, "I can't stop strumming until Moth
stops dancing."

"Moth," said the night wind, "will you stop dancing
   so Frog will stop strumming
      so Cricket will stop playing
         so Mockingbird will stop singing
            so the child can go to sleep?"

But Moth loved to dip and twirl on widespread wings by
moonlight.
   "Impossible," said Moth. "The night is too, too beautiful.
I can't stop dancing until Moon stops shining."

"Moon," said the night wind, "will you stop shining
so Moth will stop dancing
so Frog will stop strumming
so Cricket will stop playing
so Mockingbird will stop singing
so the child can go to sleep?"

But Moon's glow was so strong, it turned the green meadow grass to silver.

"Hard to do," said Moon, "hard to do. I can't stop shining unless there's a change in the weather."

Far to the west hovered a small dark shadow.

"Cloud," called the night wind, "will you cover the earth
so Moon will stop shining
so Moth will stop dancing
so Frog will stop strumming
so Cricket will stop playing
so Mockingbird will stop singing
so the child can go to sleep?"

"Only if you will carry me," said Cloud.

In a rush of cool air the night wind scooped up Cloud. Soon
a mist spread over the meadow. A gentle rain began to fall,
tumbling down through the dark, splashing on the flat bay
waters, skipping on the warm green earth.

Moon stopped shining.

Moth stopped dancing.

Frog stopped strumming.

Cricket stopped playing.

Mockingbird stopped singing.

At last the night was dark, and quiet, and still. The child snuggled under warm blankets, closed tired eyes, and fell asleep.

"Good night," said the wind.